The Writing on the Wall

by Dina Anastasio
illustrated by Lyn Boyer

Tia's Bad Day

by Amanda Jenkins
illustrated by Shawn Byous

TWO REALISTIC FICTION STORIES

Table of Contents

Realistic Fiction

What is realistic fiction?

Realistic fiction features characters and plots that could actually happen in everyday life. The settings are authentic—they are based on familiar places such as a home, school, office, or farm. The stories involve some type of conflict, or problem. The conflict can be something a character faces within himself, an issue between characters, or a problem between a character and nature.

What is the purpose of realistic fiction?

Realistic fiction shows how people grow and learn, deal with successes and failures, make decisions, build relationships, and solve problems. In addition to making readers think and wonder, realistic fiction is entertaining. Most of us enjoy "escaping" into someone else's life for a while.

How do you read realistic fiction?

First, note the title. The title will give you a clue about an important character or conflict in the story. As you read, pay attention to the thoughts, feelings, and actions of the main characters. Note how the characters change from the beginning of the story to the end. Ask yourself: *What moves this character to action? Can I learn something from his or her struggles?*

Features of Realistic Fiction

The story takes place in an authentic setting.

At least one character deals with a conflict (self, others, or nature).

The characters are like people you might meet in real life.

The story is told from a first-person or third-person point of view.

Who tells the story in realistic fiction?

Authors usually write realistic fiction in one of two ways. In the first-person point of view, one of the characters tells the story as it happens to him or her, using words such as **I**, **me**, **my**, **mine**, **we**, **us**, and **our**. In the third-person point of view, a narrator tells the story, using words such as **he**, **she**, **they**, **their**, and the proper names of the characters.

Meet the Characters

Cave Adventures

Summer has finally arrived. Linda and her brother Jake have been coming to the same cabin on this rocky beach since they were little. Their friend Maria is back for her second summer. Cai is new to the seacoast. This summer promises new adventures since Linda and Jake's dad recently discovered a hidden cave.

Linda, 12, is a big talker with big ideas. She loves technology and gadgets, and hates that the cabins do not get TV reception or the Internet.

Jake, 11, is a smart boy who enjoys playing tricks and shooting hoops on the basket outside the cabin.

Maria, 10, is an only child. She lives with her divorced mother. She likes to bake and cook, and usually has her nose in a book.

Cai, 11, is spending the summer with his grandma. He likes to swim, fish, and play with his dog Tucker.

Oak Street Kids

Five kids couldn't be more different than Jalissa, Jamal, Brooke, Luke, and Tia. But they have some things in common, too! They all live in the Oak Street Apartments. They all have parents who work during the day. They are in the same afterschool "club" run by the manager of the apartment building, Ms. Tilly. That's why the Oak Street Kids have made a deal: They will always stick together and help one another.

Jalissa, 10, likes drama and excitement, and is Jamal's twin sister.

Jamal, 10, is calm and easygoing, the opposite of his twin sister.

Brooke, 11, can always be counted on to organize and take charge.

Luke, 11, may not be a top student, but he's loyal and fun.

Tia, 9, loves every kind of sport.

Ms. Tilly is the no-nonsense manager of the Oak Street Apartments and takes care of the kids after school.

5

The Writing on the Wall

My mother was braiding my hair in the kitchen of our cabin. "Maria! I have something to tell you!" my friend Jake called from outside. It sounded important.

"Mom, are you done yet?" I asked, fidgeting.

Mom secured the last braid with a rubber band. Then she patted the top of my head. "You're done," she smiled. "But don't forget."

"Forget what?" I asked her.

A sad look passed over my mother's face. The moment I saw it, I remembered. Today was our morning. Mom and I had been planning it for a week. We even posted a list of things to do on the fridge.

Things to Do During Maria and Mom's
Morning at the Beach
1. Have a breakfast picnic on the big rock.
2. Find two shells that match perfectly.
3. Make a beautiful sketch in the sand with our bare feet.
4. Play Follow the Leader while we're jumping the waves near the shore.

The screen door creaked awake, then protested the disturbance by closing with a loud *CLAP!* against the doorframe as Jake rushed inside.

Jake was wearing his plaid pajama top. His red hair was a mess. His jeans were covered with a gray dust that I'd never seen before.

"Today is no **ordinary** day," my mother told Jake as she cleaned the table. "Today is a very special day. Maria and I are spending the morning together on the beach . . . just the two of us."

Mom left the kitchen. Then she poked her head back in and said, "Don't forget, dear." Her face seemed worried, like she thought I might go off with Jake. That's what I wanted to do, but I wouldn't do that to my mom.

As soon as my mother left the room, Jake pleaded, "You have to come to the cave, Maria! Right now! I have the most incredible surprise to show you!"

I tried to act uninterested, but I must admit that I was **curious**. Jake's father had discovered the cave a week ago. Jake loved it there. Linda, Cai, and I all loved the cave, too. It was our own private fortress. We were going to meet up there later.

"You can show me the incredible surprise this afternoon," I said. "This morning is my time with my mom."

"It won't take long," Jake begged. "I promise."

It occurred to me that Jake might have a trick in mind. I didn't care, because his tricks never hurt anyone or made people feel sad or foolish.

Jake was pleading. "*Please* come with me now."

I could hear my mother walking back and forth upstairs. She was whistling as she got ready for our special morning. She sounded very happy up there.

I didn't want to hurt my mother's feelings. I didn't want to hurt Jake's feelings, either. Plus, I really wanted to see what Jake had found.

Maybe I could make them both happy. The cave wasn't far from my cabin. If Jake and I ran very fast, I could be back before my mother came downstairs. She might not even know I was gone.

"We have to hurry," I told Jake as I raced through the doorway and leaped down the porch steps.

The rays from the morning sun darted into the cave opening, lighting up the walls inside. "Okay," I said. "Show me. But hurry." I was beginning to feel nervous. What if Mom went downstairs to pack our picnic basket and couldn't find me?

We went inside. Jake pointed to the cave wall. Someone had carved a stick figure of a girl. The girl had her arms in the air.

"Isn't it great!" he shouted. "I'll bet that piece of art was created thousands of years ago. It's definitely an **ancient** carving."

"Maybe," I said. I took out my flashlight and pointed it at the girl. The carving did look a lot like the ancient cave art that I'd seen in books. The circular head had no eyes, nose, or mouth. The five fingers on each of the hands above her head were spread out wide. Her long hair was in braids, with circles that looked like . . . rubber bands?

"That girl looks just like you, Maria!" Jake shouted from behind me. His words echoed, which must have frightened him, because he didn't speak for a while. "Maybe you have an ancient twin," he finally **whispered**.

I thought about the girl on the wall. Did I really have an ancient twin who wore her hair in braids like me? Did she jump waves and play Follow the Leader at the shore? Did she have picnic breakfasts on the big rock? Did she keep her mother waiting?

I moved toward the cave opening. "I have to go," I told Jake.

"What about your ancient twin?"

"I don't have an ancient twin," I said. "I have a modern-day twin. Ancient twins don't wear rubber bands. And Jake?"

Jake was shuffling his feet. He was staring at the floor of the cave, looking guilty. I pointed my light. The floor was covered with gray dust. The beam from the flashlight spied the pointed stone that Jake was trying to kick away.

"Next time, wash the stone dust off your jeans after you're finished carving 'ancient' pictures on the walls," I said. Then I gave a little laugh.

"You can borrow my flashlight in case you want to stay here and rework your carving." I said good-bye and raced home.

Mom was sitting at the kitchen table with her back to the door. Her shoulders seemed to be frowning. That made me a little sad, too. She didn't hear me come in. The empty picnic basket was on the table. I opened the refrigerator and took out the food that we had prepared last night.

When the food was packed in the basket I said, "I'm sorry, Mom. I shouldn't have left, even for a minute. I hope you will accept my apology. I also hope that you will be willing to change our plans. Instead of spending the morning together . . . let's spend the whole day together."

Mom didn't say anything. She just hugged me and took my hand. We walked away from the cabins and the cave, and headed to the big rock where we liked to watch the waves wash ashore.

The morning sun followed us, smiling brightly.

Reread the Story

Analyze the Characters, Setting, and Plot
- Who were the characters in the story?
- Where and when does the story take place?
- Which character is telling the story?
- What was the main character's problem?
- What do you think Jake might do next?

Analyze the Tools Writers Use: Personification
Find examples of personification in the story.
- Did the screen door really wake up? What did the author mean? (page 7)
- How did Mom's shoulders express her feelings? What did the author mean? (page 11)
- How did the morning sun express its feelings? What else might the author have said? (page 12)

Focus on Words: Antonyms
Antonyms are words that have opposite meanings. For example, in this story **definitely** and **maybe** are antonyms. Antonyms can help you define unfamiliar words. Make a chart like the one below. Then reread the story to find antonyms for the following words.

Page	Word	Antonym	How do you know?
7	ordinary		
8	curious		
10	ancient		
10	whispered		

Tia's Bad Day

Tia knew that it was going to be a bad day. First she overslept. So she had to rush to get ready for school. She sprinted down the stairs and found Jamal, Jalissa, Brooke, and Luke waiting for her.

"Sorry I'm late again," Tia apologized.

"It's all right," Jamal replied. "We can still make it on time if we hurry. No **dawdling**!"

They ran all the way to school. Tia slid into her seat just before the tardy bell rang.

Soon it was time for math class. "Oh no!" said Tia, smacking herself in the forehead. "I was rushing and left my work at home! But I did do it, Ms. Parsons! I promise I did!"

"I believe you, Tia," said Ms. Parsons. "I'll let you turn it in tomorrow. But I have to **record** a zero. When you turn in the homework, I'll erase the zero and give you a grade."

Tia had never received a zero before, not even for a split second. Now she knew for sure that it was going to be a bad day. She wasn't surprised when another bad thing happened at lunchtime.

"Rats!" Tia groaned. "I forgot my lunch, too!" She knew she wouldn't go hungry because the cafeteria lady would give her a free sandwich. But the free sandwich was always peanut butter. Yuck! Peanut butter was gooey. It stuck to the roof of her mouth. Tia only managed to eat half of her sandwich before her tongue refused to touch any more of it.

"This has been a terrible day," she told the other Oak Street kids that afternoon as they walked home from school.

"Be glad that you can get that zero erased," Brooke consoled her. "My teacher won't take late work at all."

"I like peanut butter," Luke said wistfully, "I wish that I'd forgotten *my* lunch."

As soon as they got back to the apartments, the other kids opened their backpacks. The building manager, Ms. Tilly, watched the kids after school. Ms. Tilly had a rule: no playing until all of your homework was done.

Brooke started typing a book report. Luke corrected his math test. Jamal studied spelling. Jalissa did a worksheet. Everyone but Tia had homework.

Tia got her football. She wanted to practice her forward pass, but she couldn't throw a football to herself. She sat in a chair and waited for one of the other kids to finish. Sitting around was boring. Tia was glad when Jalissa put her worksheet away.

"Will you throw the football with me?" Tia asked.

"Sorry, but no," Jalissa replied, pulling out three bottles of fingernail polish. "Tomorrow I'm leading my class in the Pledge of Allegiance, so I'm going to paint my fingernails red, white, and blue!"

Tia slumped in her chair. "What an awful day," she muttered to herself.

"I'm done!" Luke announced, slapping his math folder shut.

Luke spent as little time as possible on homework. "I'll play with you, Tia."

They went outside to the apartment courtyard. Tia knew they'd have to be **careful** with the football. Many of the patios were decorated with flowerpots and wind chimes. One careless throw could mean broken pottery or glass.

They had been outside for only three tosses when Luke said, "I'm hungry. Let's get a snack."

"No!" said Tia. "Let's keep playing."

"But I'm starving," Luke protested. "I want a peanut butter sandwich!" He turned and started across the courtyard.

"This is the worst day ever!" Tia shouted.

> The author uses both description and dialogue to develop the characters and their relationships.

Tia saw Brooke, Jamal, and Jalissa coming out to play. But now she was too mad to stop herself from angrily punting the football.

PONK! The ball jumped off her foot. It shot toward a nearby patio and a hanging pot of red flowers. *CRASH!* The pot shattered. Dirt and flowers flew everywhere. Broken pieces of pottery hit the ground and danced off in all directions.

Luke whirled around. "Whoa!" he said, wide-eyed.

"Those are Mr. Morgan's flowers!" Jamal said.

"Those *were* Mr. Morgan's flowers," Luke corrected.

The five kids crept over to inspect the damage. "The poor things!" said Jalissa, looking at the limp blossoms.

"I can't tell Mr. Morgan!" Tia wailed. "He'll be furious!"

"You *have* to tell him," said Brooke.

"Don't worry," Jamal assured Tia. "We'll come with you."

Tia knew that they were right. "Let's get it over with," she said as she gloomily knocked on Mr. Morgan's door.

When the door opened, Tia said in a rush, "I'm sorry, Mr. Morgan, but I— I broke one of your flowerpots."

The author uses personification to describe what happens to the pieces of the pot after they hit the ground.

Mr. Morgan stepped onto the patio to look. "Boy, you sure did!" he said, eyeing the mess. "I think most of the flowers will be all right if I replant them quickly. I just need to make room in some of these other pots."

"M-may I help you?" Tia said, still nervous.

"Sure," said Mr. Morgan.

"We'll help, too," Brooke decided. "Jalissa and I will pick up the broken pieces. Jamal, you and Luke please sweep up the dirt." They all set to work.

"I'm sorry that I destroyed your pot," Tia told Mr. Morgan as she handed him a flower, soil clinging to its roots.

Mr. Morgan worked the red flower in next to a yellow one. "That's a **negative** way of looking at it," he said. "Let's look at the positive side. No one was hurt. And at least you didn't break my window!"

"I'll save my allowance," Tia told him. "I'll buy you a new pot as soon as I can."

"Thank you for the offer," said Mr. Morgan. "But I think the flowers look better this way. The pots are fuller and more colorful."

Here the author presents another conflict to keep readers engaged. Will Mr. Morgan be angry at Tia for breaking his flowerpot?

The author develops the characters' personalities and their relationships by showing how they work together to help a friend.

The main character solves the problem she is having with herself. Tia learns that attitude is often determined by what we pay attention to. Readers can enjoy the humor in the story, and can also relate to the ending.

Suddenly Tia felt very lucky. Just minutes ago, she had been in a terrible mood because of all the bad things that had happened. Now she was relieved and glad!

"The only thing that's different," she thought, "is that now I'm focusing on good things, like Mr. Morgan being nice to me and my friends helping me out."

At first, the replanted flowers **sagged** a little. But as Mr. Morgan watered them, they perked up and turned their faces to the sun.

"You know what, Mr. Morgan?" Tia said. "I think this bad day is going to end up being pretty **fantastic**!"

Reread the Story

Analyze the Characters, Setting, and Plot
- Who were the characters in the story?
- Where and when does the story take place?
- Is the story written in the first-person point of view or the third-person point of view? How do you know?
- What was the main character's problem?
- What relationships does the main character have with the other characters? How do those relationships affect the outcome of the story?

Analyze the Tools Writers Use: Personification
Find examples of personification in this story when:
- Tia can only eat half of her sandwich. (page 15)
- Tia angrily punts the football. (page 18)
- Broken pieces of pottery hit the ground. (page 18)
- Mr. Morgan waters the replanted flowers. (page 20)

Focus on Words: Antonyms
Make a chart like the one below. Then look for antonyms in the story to help you understand the following words.

Page	Word	Antonym	How do you know?
14	dawdling		
15	record		
17	careful		
19	negative		
20	sagged		
20	fantastic		

How does an author write

Realistic Fiction?

Reread "Tia's Bad Day" and think about what Amanda Jenkins did to write this story. How did she develop it? How can you, as a writer, develop your own story?

1. Decide on a Problem

Remember: The characters in realistic fiction face the same problems that you might face. In "Tia's Bad Day," the problem is a girl who becomes gloomy and cranky when everything seems to go wrong.

Character	Tia	Ms. Parsons	Mr. Morgan
Traits	responsible; moody	organized; fair	forgiving; a good problem solver
Examples	She feels bad when she almost makes her friends late for school, but gets upset with them when they won't play with her.	She wants students to turn in to their homework on time, but has a back-up system in case someone forgets.	He doesn't want Tia to feel bad about the flowers, and proposes a plan to save them.

2. Brainstorm Characters
Writers ask these questions:

- What kind of person will my main character be? What are his or her traits? Interests?

- What things are important to my main character? What does he or she want?

- What other characters will be important to my story? How will each one help or hinder the main character?

- How will the characters change? What will they learn about life?

3. Brainstorm Setting and Plot
Writers ask these questions:

- Where does my story take place? How will I describe the setting?

- What is the problem, or situation?

- What events happen? How does the story end?

- Will my readers be entertained? Will they learn something?

Setting	Oak Street Apartments
Problem of the Story	A girl is upset because everything about her day is going wrong.
Story Events	1. The girl oversleeps and is almost late for school. 2. She forgets her math homework and lunch. 3. She becomes angry at her friends, kicks a football into her neighbor's patio, and breaks one of his flowerpots.
Solution to the Problem	The teacher gives the girl an extra day to bring in her homework. The cafeteria lady gives her a peanut butter sandwich to eat. The neighbor accepts her help in cleaning up the mess and repotting the plant. The girl decides the day will be good after all.

Glossary

ancient (ANE-shunt) very old (page 10)

careful (KAIR-ful) cautious (page 17)

curious (KYER-ee-us) interested in investigating new things (page 8)

dawdling (DAU-duh-ling) wasting time (page 14)

fantastic (fan-TAS-tik) excellent (page 20)

negative (NEH-guh-tiv) lacking positivity (page 19)

ordinary (OR-dih-nair-ee) routine; normal (page 7)

record (rih-KORD) to make a written note (page 15)

sagged (SAGD) drooped (page 20)

whispered (WIS-perd) spoke very softly, especially so as not to be heard (page 10)